E. P. Dutton and Company

Sunshine

E. P. Dutton and Company

Sunshine

ISBN/EAN: 9783337254957

Printed in Europe, USA, Canada, Australia, Japan

Cover: Foto ©Andreas Hilbeck / pixelio.de

More available books at **www.hansebooks.com**

" Unto you that fear My Name, shall the Sun of Righteousness arise, with healing in his wings."

UNSHINE.

" Oh, timely happy, timely wise,
Hearts that with rising morn arise."

" New mercies each returning day,
Hover around us while we pray."

" Day unto day uttereth speech."

And to the Christian heart, however, weary,
There comes no sorrow Jesus will not share.
Nor holds wide earth a spot so sad and dreary,
But, Sun of Righteousness, Thou shinest there

E. P. DUTTON AND COMPANY,
NEW YORK: 718 BROADWAY.
1878.

Dedication.

◆

To my dear friend,

J. E. B.

This little volume is affectionately dedicated, in loving remembrance of the happy hours of "Sunshine" and "Starlight" we have spent together, and with an earnest hope that in the future world we may find that

> E'en as the cup which skillful hand
> Hath filled till but one small drop more
> Would cause its overflow, — yet safe
> A rose-leaf on its surface bore,
> Thus in our souls, the fount of bliss
> Made *perfect in Christ's presence*, — by
> His grace has added blessing bears, —
> *Friendship throughout eternity.*

M. H S

Sunshine.

1st *Day*.

"His compassions fail not, they are new every morning."

NOT only are God's *blessings* new every morning, but His *compassions* "fail not"! He is indeed "very pitiful, and of tender mercy." And although I may grieve Him day by day by my waywardness, yet He will bring me back to His side; His loving voice will recall me; He will say, "Come unto Me, O weary and heavy-laden."

"New every morning is the love
   Our waking and up-rising prove!
   Through sleep and darkness safely
     brought,
   Restored to life, and power, and
     thought."

Blessed Lord, make me so wholly Thine that I cannot thus abuse Thy wonderful love and unfailing compassion : may Thy *goodness* lead me this day to repentance, and Thy Holy Spirit so abide with me that I may glorify Thee in thought, word, and deed, for my dear Saviour's sake.   AMEN.

"Whatsoever ye do in word or deed, do all in the Name of the Lord Jesus."

IF we would indeed "do all in the Name of the Lord Jesus," how blessed a day this would be : with every energy of mind and soul bent to heavenward aims, to glorifying God, to purifying ourselves from sin, it would truly be a day nearer Heaven. Let me then bear constantly in mind whose I am ; let me strive to be " hidden in Christ," and to lead others to " Behold the Lamb of God."

— ◆ —

"Wherever in the world I am,
   In whatsoe'er estate,
I have fellowship with other hearts
   To seek and cultivate,
And a work of lowly love to do
   For the Lord on whom I wait."

— ◆ —

" Direct us, O Lord, by Thy most gracious favor, and further us with Thy continual help, that in all our works begun, continued, and ended in Thee, we may glorify Thy Holy Name, and finally through Thy mercy obtain everlasting life, through Jesus Christ our Lord."   Amen.

"In all thy ways acknowledge Him, and He
shall direct thy paths."

LET us strive this one day to remember Christ, and not be ashamed to acknowledge Him either to ourselves or to others. Let all "take knowledge of us, that we have been with Jesus." Let us *live* Christ even more than we speak of Him, but if necessary boldly confess that we are His soldiers and servants. His soldiers, because we are to fight on His side; His servants, in that we are entirely dependent upon Him.

———◆———

"His love doth follow my steps, but I
    Am a poor sinner and no more!
The Lord my Shepherd He is the same,
He doth not measure His love by
    mine.
True and unchangeable is His Name,
His love and pity are all Divine!
He doth remember though I forget,
And therefore I think He'll keep me
    yet."

"O God, the Protector of all that trust in Thee, without whom nothing is strong, nothing is holy, grant that Thou being our Ruler and Guide, we may so pass through things temporal that we finally lose not the things eternal, through Jesus our Lord." AMEN.

"Pray without ceasing." "He ever liveth to make intercession for them."

JESUS is always near us, and we may always lift our hearts to Him in prayer, and He will plead for us before our Father. Wonderful compassion! the Son of God pleading our feeble petitions! Through Him alone can we hope to secure an answer to our prayers, but if we only ask *believing*, all things shall be given unto us.

———◆———

"Go when the morning shineth,
    Go when the noon is bright,
Go when the eve declineth,
    Go in the hush of night:
Go with pure thought and feeling,
    Fling earthly thought away,
And in thy closet kneeling,
    Do thou in secret pray."

———◆———

"O Thou who art always more ready to hear than we to pray, and art wont to give more than either we desire or deserve," bless us this day for our dear Saviour's sake. AMEN.

"**Bear ye one another's burdens, and so fulfil the law of Christ.**"

IF thus we strive to bless others, we shall surely be blessed ourselves. Let us first of all work and pray for our fellow-beings, and then some one's prayers will be answered for *us*. Let us this day make some one happy, and begin *right around* us; not looking away for some great thing to accomplish, but taking the duty *nearest* to us, do *that*, and then we shall see the *next*. In little things we can thus do much for Christ, though still "more careful than to serve Him much, to please Him perfectly."

———◆———

"I ask Thee for a thoughtful love
   Through constant watching wise,
To meet the glad with joyful smiles
   And to wipe the weeping eyes;
And a heart at leisure from itself
   To soothe and sympathize."

———◆———

O Thou who hast taught us that as Thou hast loved us, so ought we also to love one another, grant unto us grace to follow Thy blessed example, Who didst die upon the cross that we might live, that we may this day and always endeavor to love our neighbor as ourselves. We ask it for Jesus' sake. AMEN.

"**All things work together for good, to them
that love God.**"

DID we really believe this, how differ-
ently we should bear the trials of
life. However heavy the cross, we should
willingly take it up, knowing who hath
laid it upon us. However sharp the
bereavement, we should feel that "the
Lord gave and the Lord hath taken
away." However sore the temptation,
we should cry "Get thee behind me, Sa-
tan," and looking unto Jesus, be saved.
Yes, all things work together for good to
those who *love God*. See to it then, O
my soul, that thou lovest Him, that thus
this promise may be fulfilled to thee.

———◆———

"Oh! there is nothing in the world
   To weigh against Thy will!
E'en the dark times I dread the most
   Thy covenant fulfill,
And when the pleasant morning dawns,
   I find Thee with me still."

———◆———

Dear Jesus, to obtain that which Thou
dost promise, make us to love that which

Thou dost command, and to trust Thy infinite compassion, which doeth all things well. Grant it for Thine own sake. Amen.

'Cast thy burden on the Lord, and He shall
sustain thee."

AN humble child-like spirit is what I
would especially cultivate to-day.
How happy I should be if like a little
child I could with one hand "hold fast
by my Father" all the day long, while,
with my other hand I "pluck the flowers
along the pathway of life."

———◆———

"What Thou shalt to-day provide,
    Let me as a child receive;
What to-morrow may betide
    Calmly to Thy wisdom leave.
'Tis enough that *Thou* wilt care;
    Why should I the burden bear?"

———◆———

Blessed Jesus, who for our sakes didst
humble Thyself to become a little child,
grant unto us that spirit of meekness
which Thou didst manifest, and help us in
all things to glorify our Heavenly Father,
for Thy own Name's sake. AMEN.

Whom have I in Heaven but Thee? and there is none upon earth that I desire besides Thee!"

IF we would be happy in this transitory life, we must love God supremely; no earthly friend, however dear, must fill *His* place within our hearts. Yet if we seek earnestly to be filled with love toward Him, then we need not fear that He will chide us for loving our dear ones, since He has said, "As I have loved you, so also should ye love one another."

———◆———

'Source of my life's refreshing springs,
　　Whose presence in my heart sustains me,
Thy love appoints me pleasant things,
　　Thy mercy orders all that pains me!
If loving hearts were never lonely,
　　If all they wish might always be,
Accepting what they look for only,
　　They might be glad, but not in Thee!"

———◆———

Gracious Lord, whose Name is Love,
2

teach us to make Thee first in our hearts, that thus we fall not into condemnation. We ask it for Thy Well-Beloved's sake, Jesus Christ our Saviour.   AMEN.

"The beloved of the Lord shall dwell in safety by Him." "All his saints are in Thy Hand."

HOW comforting to the Christian's heart are the *Names* by which God calls His people. "The Beloved of the Lord;" oh, what a glorious title is that! May it be said of us as of Daniel, "O man greatly beloved, fear nɔt! peace be unto thee! be strong, yea be strong!" and again, — "At the beginning of thy supplications the commandment came forth, and I am come to shew thee: for thou art *greatly beloved.*"

———◆———

"Under Thy wings, my God, I rest!
　Under Thy shadow safely lie,
By Thy own strength in peace pos-
　　sessed,
　While dreaded evils pass me by!
My place of lowly service too,
　Beneath Thy sheltering wings I see,
For all the work I have to do,
　Is done through strengthening rest
　　in Thee."

Our Father in Heaven, grant us this day and always to live as becometh our calling as Thy Beloved, that thus we may be saved both in body and soul, for our Blessed Jesus' sake. AMEN.

"Thou wilt keep him in perfect peace, whose mind is stayed on Thee!"

IN "perfect peace:" can I indeed thus be kept even when sorrows press heavily upon me, or when all seems dark and dreary? Yes, — but *God* must keep us in it: we cannot sustain ourselves in it; but if we stay our minds upon *Him* as our Rock of Salvation, if we trust wholly to the Omniscient Eye which seeth what is best for us, then indeed shall we be kept in "perfect peace."

———◆———

"Oh! this is blessing, this is rest —
    Into Thine arms, O Lord, I flee:
I hide me in Thy faithful breast
    And pour out all my soul to Thee."

———◆———

"O God, from whom all holy desires, all good counsels, and all just works do proceed, give unto Thy servants that peace which the world cannot give, that our hearts may be set to obey Thy commandments, through Christ our Lord." AMEN.

"Whatsoever thy hand findeth to do, do it
with thy might."

IF we could live each day as though it
were our last, how careful should we
be to improve every moment: how little
danger there would be of our *wasting*
any: yet we know not but this *may* be
the last!   Oh, then, why are we not
more in *earnest?*   May God forgive our
trifling away His precious time in world-
liness or sin.   Let us then ever "be
prayerful, — Heaven is won by prayer;
be sober, — for we are not there!"

———◆———

" One by one thy duties meet thee,
    Let thy whole strength go to each :
Let no future dreams elate thee,
    Learn thou first what these can teach.
Every hour that fleets so slowly
    Has its task to do, or bear :
Luminous the crown and holy,
    If we set each gem with care."

———◆———

"O Thou who hast safely brought us

to the beginning of this day, defend us in the same by Thy mighty power, and grant that this day we fall into no sin, for our Redeemer's sake." AMEN.

"I count all things but loss, for the excellency of the knowledge of Christ Jesus our Lord."

THIS is a "hard saying" for our weak human hearts. We cling to pleasure and luxury, — we do not often "count all things but loss" for Jesus' sake, but we must endeavor to "seek first the kingdom of God;" then we may with a good conscience enjoy such earthly blessings as He may "add unto us."

———◆———

"Though some good things of lower worth
　　My heart is called on to resign,
Of all the gifts in Heaven or earth,
　　The greatest and the best is mine.
The love of God in Christ made known,
The love that is enough alone,
My Father's love is all my own."

———◆———

O Merciful Father who of Thy tender love towards mankind, didst send Thy only Son Jesus Christ to suffer death, that we might live, teach us so to value this inestimable benefit, that we may show forth our gratitude not only with our lips but in our lives, that at last we obtain that other precious gift of eternal life through His merits, our Lord and Saviour Jesus Christ.   AMEN.

"There is therefore now no condemnation, to
them which are in Christ Jesus."

"HIDDEN in Christ," even God's Omniscient Eye can see naught but *His* likeness, and therefore He can love us, and welcome us as His children through this "Well-Beloved." Hidden there the law cannot condemn us, "for whom Christ died."

O my soul! is it indeed true that all thy wretchedness and guilt have been washed away "through His most precious blood?" Then indeed shouldst thou "rejoice and be exceeding glad."

—◆—

"My soul's Restorer, let me learn
    In Thy deep love to live and rest!
Let me the precious thing discern
    Of which I am indeed possessed.
My treasure let me feel and see,
And let my moments as they flee
Unfold my endless life in Thee!"

—◆—

"We therefore pray Thee help Thy

servants, whom Thou hast redeemed with Thy precious blood. Vouchsafe O Lord to keep us this day without sin." Amen.

" **Whosoever shall do the will of my Father which is in Heaven, the same is my brother, and sister, and mother.**"

ALL Christians are "one in Christ Jesus." How strong and tender the tie which should bind them together. Let me see to it this day that neither in thought, word, or deed may I "hurt one of these little ones." Let me rather help some weary brother in the way of life, and be ready always to "be pitiful and courteous."

'T is not that in our veins we trace
    One drop of kindred blood: the tide
Of life within our souls is one, —
    The blood which flows from Jesus' side.
Our souls have chosen the same road
    Through joy or sorrow, light or gloom.
That way is narrow: can we then
     Far separate reach our Heavenly Home?

Our Father in Heaven, who hast knit

together Thine elect in one body, grant unto me and to all my dear friends in Christ Jesus all spiritual blessings this day, for our Elder Brother's sake. AMEN.

"Be ye therefore followers of God, as dear
children, and walk in love, as Christ
also hath loved us."

"LOVE is the fulfilling of the law:"
and surely we cannot care too
tenderly for our dear ones, since God's
word bids us to love one another as He
hath loved us. *Such* love indeed we
cannot attain unto, but we can strive
after it.

———◆———

"Our sweet and holy union
   Knows neither time nor place;
The love which God hath planted
   Is lasting as His grace.
We tread one path to glory,
   Are guided by one Hand,
And led in faith and patience
   Unto one Father-land."

———◆———

Grant, Blessed Jesus, that we, loving
Thee above all others, may love our
neighbors as ourselves, and daily minis-
ter unto them for Thy sake, O precious
Saviour, who didst lay down Thy life for
our sake. AMEN.

"I pray not that Thou shouldest take them out of the world, but that Thou shouldest keep them from the evil."

JESUS, our great Example, was rarely left alone in communion with God — only as He spent whole nights in prayer, an example poor human nature is loth to follow.

But often to us, when we seem to see Him face to face, and that it is indeed good for us to be there, comes a summons to the duties of life, which would seem irksome did we not remember our Lord's own words to His disciples, — "Arise, let us go hence : " and again His precious words, — "I pray not that Thou shouldest take them out of the world, *but* that Thou shouldest keep them from the evil."

———◆———

"I ask Thee for the daily strength
　　To none who ask denied ;
For a mind to blend with outward life
　　While keeping at Thy side,
Content to fill a little space
　　So *Thou* be glorified."

Keep us, O Lord, by Thy mighty power, from all the temptations which daily beset us, that we may shine in the world as Thy followers should. Be Thou our Intercessor that we may be kept from *all evil;* and be our Merciful Saviour both now and ever. AMEN.

"Ask, and ye shall receive."

OH, for a stronger faith in God's promises to hear and to answer prayer ! Whatsoever we shall ask, be it little things or great, we shall *receive* them. Not always perhaps, just in the way we have asked for them, but if we *watch* as well as pray, we shall find the answer. And not only at morning and at night, but all through the day let my heart be asking blessings at God's Hand. "We are coming to a *King*," "Large petitions let us bring."

———◆———

"My God, is any hour so sweet
　　From blush of morn to evening star,
As that which calls me to Thy feet,
　　The hour of prayer !
Blest is that tranquil hour of morn,
　　And blest that hour of solemn eve,
When on the wings of faith up-borne,
　　The world I leave !

———◆———

O Gracious Spirit, Who alone canst change our vile hearts and make them

3

fit dwelling-places for the Saviour, teach us to ask for such things as Thou seest we need, for the sake of Him who ever liveth to make intercession for us. AMEN.

'If any man sin, we have an Advocate with
the Father, Jesus Christ the righteous,
and He is the propitiation for
our sins."

HOW humbly should we walk all the
day, could we but realize the suf-
ferings we cost our Saviour, even amid
the glory of Heaven, by our sinfulness!
To remember that *Jesus* is watching us,
and that our every thought is read by
Him, should keep us from every temptation to evil. To look *backward* to the
cross, and *onward* to the *crown*, should
so occupy our minds that the vanities of
earth should be easily passed, on our
daily road.

———◆———

"Oh for a heart to praise my God,
　　A heart from sin set free!
A heart that always feels the blood
　　So freely shed for me!
A heart resigned, submissive, meek,
　　My dear Redeemer's throne,
Where only Christ is heard to speak,
　　Where Jesus reigns alone."

"Grant, O Lord, that by continually mortifying our corrupt affections we may purify ourselves even as Christ is pure, and be made like unto Him in all things, to whom be honor and glory world without end." AMEN.

'I will lift up mine eyes unto the hills from whence cometh my help.''

UPON the "Everlasting Hills" walks my Saviour, yet notes each event in the life of His humblest follower. Unto Him then will I look each hour of this day for sympathy in my joys or sorrows, my sickness or my health. His gracious love is mine, if only I claim it, and naught can harm one clad in *that* armor. "Accepted in the Beloved." Let this thought keep me in peace all the day, and let me be ever looking unto Him "from whence cometh my help."

———◆———

"My Jesus as Thou wilt!
    All shall be well for me,
Each changing future scene
    I gladly trust with Thee!
Straight to my Home above,
    I travel calmly on,
And sing, in life or death,
    My Lord, Thy will be done."

O God, amid all the changes and chances of this mortal life, ever defend us by Thy continued and ready help, through Jesus Christ our Lord. AMEN.

"**My grace is sufficient for thee.**"

HOWEVER weak, through sin or from sorrow, we may be, we have God's precious promise, that His grace will be *sufficient* for us. The "grace of God!" ah! through this we can indeed "do all things." "The grace of our Lord Jesus Christ be with you;" how often, and how carelessly have I responded "Amen" to this petition; yet how full of wonderful promise it is. "Sufficient" for *every* emergency, however sudden. Even if we seem entering "Death's dark valley," that grace can either bring us back to life, or sustain as through the shadows on into the Sunshine of Jesus' presence.

———◆———

" Shall I not trust my God,
  Who doth so well love me?
  Who as a Father cares so tenderly?
  Shall I not lay the load
  Which would my weakness break,
  On His strong Hand who never doth
    forsake?"

O God, who knowest us to be set in the midst of so many and great dangers, give us such faith in Thee that we may trust Thine all-sufficient grace, which Thou hast given us in Christ our Saviour, all our lives long. AMEN.

"All the paths of the Lord are mercy and
truth unto such as keep His covenant
and His testimonies."

POOR human wisdom is often baffled
in the paths it marks out for itself.
The hand of God hedges up the way,
and we turn aside, and wonder. Let us
try simply to *trust* our Father, and walk
in the way of His commandment, then
shall we never go astray.

———◆———

" What cheering words are these,
    Their sweetness who can tell ?
In time and to eternal days,
    'T is with the righteous well !
'T is well with them while life endures,
    And well when called to die."

———◆———

"O Merciful God, who knowest that
we have no power of ourselves to help
ourselves, so order our unruly wills and
affections that we may run the way of
Thy commandments, and desire those
things which Thou dost promise,"
through Jesus Christ our Lord. AMEN.

"When my spirit was overwhelmed within me, then Thou knewest my path."

GOD'S Omniscient Eye knows our path, even "from the beginning;" so, however dark it may be to us, it is all light to Him. Our spirit may be "overwhelmed" with joy or with sorrow; but through either, our Father's Eye detects the course we shall take, the way we shall choose. Again, the lesson is, "Trust Him."

———◆———

"My sorrowing friend arise, and go
    About thy house with patient care;
The Hand that bows thy head so low
    Will *bear* the ills thou canst not bear.
Arise, and all thy tasks fulfill,
    And 'as thy day, thy strength shall
      be!'
Were there not *power* beyond the ill,
    The ill would not have come to thee.
Though cloud and storm encompass
      thee,
    Be not afflicted nor afraid:
Thou knowest the shadow would not
      be,
    Were there no sun beyond the shade."

Be Thou, O Jesus, our pillar of cloud by day, and of fire by night, to lead us through this wilderness-world. Then indeed we need fear no evil, for *Thou* art with us. We ask it for Thine own Name's sake. AMEN.

"I, even I, am He that comforteth you."

O WONDROUS Christ, who art the comfort of so many weary hearts! the Saviour of the world! Jesus the Crucified! this day take full possession of my soul; let it lean on Thee, and hope in Thee, and trust *to* Thee for all it is, and all it hopes to be."

———◆———

" I journey through a desert drear and
        wild,
    Yet is my heart by such sweet thoughts
        beguiled
    Of Him on whom I lean, my strength,
        my stay,
    I can forget the sorrows of the way.
                    Christ comforts me.

"Thoughts of His love, the Root of
        every grace,
    Which finds in this poor heart a dwell-
        ing-place,

The sunshine of my soul, than day
more bright,
And my calm pillow of repose by night.
Christ comforts me!"

———◆———

"O Lamb of God, who takest away
the sins of the world, receive *our* prayer."

"Our Father, which art in Heaven."

"OUR Father," the glorious God of Heaven, calls us, poor worms of the dust, His *children*. Yes, within us is a germ of immortality which fits us to be "sons of God," "joint heirs with Christ." Oh, with so great incentive as this to be *like* our Father, how pure and holy should be our lives, that we may dwell with Him at last in Heaven. Through faith in Christ we may indeed say " Abba, Father."

———◆———

" O   Father-Eye   that   hath   so   truly
    watched,
    O Father-Hand that hath so gently
    led,
    O Father-Heart that by my prayer is
    touched,
        That loved it first when it was cold
        and dead :
    Still lead me on, dear Lord, with faith-
    ful care,
        The narrow path to Heaven where I
        would go ;

And train me for the life that waits me
    there,
Alike through love and loss, through
    weal and woe."

———◆———

"O God, the Father of Heaven, have
mercy upon us, miserable sinners."
"We beseech Thee to hear us, good
Lord."

"My God shall supply all your need, accord-
ing to His riches in glory by Christ
Jesus."

"ALL my need!" oh, what a wonderful promise is this, as fitting to
our temporal as our eternal "need."
But the wonder departs when we see
what is the treasury whence God draws
all these gifts, — the riches of the glory
of His grace through Christ Jesus! oh,
there is *more* than enough for the need
of a million worlds!

———◆———

Cast thou away each doubt and fear,
Solace thy heart, dry every tear;
Comfort, and health, and strength are here,
　　　Hither, O weary, look!

For "Wisdom," my Omniscience plead,
For "Righteousness," my perfect deed,
For "Holiness," yea, all you need,
　　　To Me, O sinner, look!

———◆———

　Show us, O Lord, the secret of Thy
Grace! Show us the face of Jesus, that

we need not wonder Thou canst redeem us through Him, and break our cold, hard hearts, and hew from them living temples fit for His presence. We ask it for His Name's sake. Amen.

4

"The Lord is very pitiful, and of tender mercy."

"VERY pitiful" and of "tender mercy." Such are the attributes of my gracious Heavenly Friend. Let me not murmur then, even when I am "rebuked of Him;" for He doth not "willingly afflict or grieve the children of men." Let me trust me in His mercy, and stay my soul upo., His tender pity.

———◆———

"Yes, Lord, 'tis of Thy power alone to-
      day
    That still I draw my living breath;
    Thy grace preserves me still from
      death;
  O Father-Heart, reject me not, but stay
    With me to-day.

"Bless all my works and ways, my light
      increase,
    Order my doings for the best;
    In all my toil be Thou my rest,
  Until at last I lay me down in peace
    That cannot cease."

"O Father of mercies, and God of all comfort, our only help in time of need, look down from Heaven, we humbly beseech Thee, behold, visit, and relieve Thy servants," for Jesus' sake. AMEN.

"If a man love Me, He will keep My words."

YES, if I truly love Jesus I shall keep
His words. If we are tenderly
bound to an earthly friend by warm af-
fection, how careful we are to fulfil their
requests, and if those requests were all
for our own benefit, how quickly we
should strive to carry them out. Surely,
then, for Him who has died for me, who
offers me pleasures forevermore, who
only asks my love that He may bestow
upon me the "peace which passeth all
understanding," I should be willing to
give up myself, yea, all that I have, to
His sweet service.

——◆——

"Here is my heart, — my God, I give it
        Thee ;
    I heard Thee call, and say,
'Not to the world, my child, but unto
        Me !'
    I heard, and will obey.
Here is love's offering to my King,
Which in glad sacrifice I bring, —
        Here is my heart !"

Grant, Blessed Jesus, that we, loving Thee above all things, may desire those things which Thou dost command, for Thine own dear Name's sake. Amen.

"Through Him, we both have access by one Spirit, unto the Father."

"THROUGH *Him*," the glorious Intercessor, who everywhere this day gathers His people's prayers, and offers them as incense before the Father's throne. All who this day have prayed for me offer their petitions in His Name, and I again for them. And by the Holy Spirit, the one Gracious "Comforter," these prayers have ascended to "Our Father." Oh, the closeness of the tie that binds Christians together, — the threefold cord! love for the Father, the Son, and the Holy Ghost. May our hearts be drawn and fastened heavenward with this sacred, blessed Bond.

———◆———

"And surely in a world like this
    So rife with woe, so scant with bliss,
    'T is something that we kneel and pray
    With loved ones near and far away."

———◆———

O Holy and Blessed Trinity, grant that all who call upon Thee faithfully may be rewarded by Thy heavenly benediction, through Thee, O Blessed Jesus, whom with the Father and Holy Spirit we glorify, world without end. AMEN.

" Let this mind be in you, which was also in Christ Jesus."

IF my soul be " hidden in Christ," I cannot but show forth His mind. Ah, it was a loving, pure, and gentle behavior; it was a mind wholly given up to deeds of compassion and kindness, never reviling, never boasting. The " Mind of Christ !" Who would not give up all this world can offer, to know that this would be their blessed portion? yet it may be *mine* if only I *let* Him save and sanctify me.

———◆———

" My hope is built on nothing less
 Than Jesus' blood and righteousness,
 I dare not trust the sweetest frame,
 But wholly lean on Jesus' Name !
 On Christ, the solid Rock, I stand !
 All other ground is sinking sand."

———◆———

O Thou who knowest us to be so sinful that we can have no good thoughts without Thee, give us the mind of

Christ, and this day and always, may
we live as those should live who have
named the Name of Christ.   We ask it
for His dear sake.   AMEN

"Whom having not seen, ye love."

THE Face of Jesus! how can we im-
agine that matchless presence! and
yet we shall "see Him as He is." Let
this solemn, wondrous thought keep me
all the day humble and prayerful, that I
may see that precious Face as that of a
Loving Saviour, as well as a righteous
Judge. *My* Jesus! oh, may His Image
be found stamped upon my heart!

———◆———

"He stays me falling, lifts me up when
    down,
      Redeems me wandering, guards from
      every foe:
Plants on my worthless brow the vic-
    tor's crown
      Which in return before His feet I
      throw,
Grieved that I cannot better grace the
    shrine
      Who deigns to own me His, as He
      is mine.
While here, alas, I know not half His
    love!

But half discern Him, and but half
    adore :
But when I meet Him in the realms
    above,
  I hope to love Him better, praise
    Him more,
And feel and tell amid the choir divine,
    How fully I am His, and He is mine."

———◆———

"Spare us, Good Lord! Thou who
hast redeemed us with Thy most precious blood."

"And so shall we ever be with the Lord."
"Wherefore comfort one another with
these words."

"FOREVER with the Lord." In life
and in death, oh, the comfort of
this "word." Soon time shall be no
longer, oh, how soon for me? It may
be that never again shall I see the morning light, or it may be that long years
intervene between me and my Father's
House.

"If life be long, I will be glad,
    That I may long obey;
If short, yet why should I be sad,
    To soar to endless day?"

———◆———

"Forever with the Lord!
    Amen! so let it be;
Life from the dead is in that word,
    'T is immortality!
Here in the body pent,
    Absent from Him I roam,
Yet nightly pitch my moving tent
    A day's march nearer home."

———◆———

"We beseech Thee, O Lord, that we,

with all those who have departed in the true faith of Thy Holy Name, may have our perfect consummation and bliss, both in body and soul, in Thy eternal and everlasting kingdom," through Christ our Lord. AMEN.

" O CHRISTIAN ! hold thou on thy steadfast way,

Still looking upward for the perfect day;

So may'st thou win to cheer earth's 'little while,'
    The Saviour's smile !

"Jesus, Thy Sun the cold, dead heart shall warm,

And quicken into life the nerveless form ;

Till in His matchless Image thou shalt shine
    With light divine !

"At evening time it shall be light."

TARLIGHT.

"Now that day has passed away,
Golden stars in bright array
Bespangle the blue sky;

"Bright and clear so would I stand,
When I hear my Lord's command,
To leave this earth and upward fly!

E. P. DUTTON AND COMPANY

NEW YORK: 713 BROADWAY.

1878.

RIVERSIDE, CAMBRIDGE:
STEREOTYPED AND PRINTED BY
H. O. HOUGHTON AND COMPANY.

Starlight.

1st Night.

"I will both lay me down in peace,
and sleep, for Thou, Lord, only
makest me dwell in safety."

"WHEN the soft dews of kindly sleep
My wearied eyelids gently steep,
Be my last thought how sweet to rest
Forever on my Saviour's breast."

"Now there was leaning on Jesus'
bosom, one of His disciples,
whom Jesus loved."

"In my Father's House are many mansions." "I go to prepare a place for you."

"ONE sweetly solemn thought
    Comes to me o'er and o'er:
I'm nearer Home to-day
    Than I've ever been before!
Nearer my Father's House
    Where the many mansions be,
Nearer the great White Throne,
    Nearer the jasper-sea."

"And there shall be no night there."

"The Eternal God is thy Refuge, and
underneath are the Everlasting
Arms."

"OFT in a dark and lonely place,
  I hush my hastened breath
To hear the comfortable words
  Thy loving Spirit saith ;
And feel my safety in Thy Hand
From every kind of death."

"I will never leave thee nor forsake
thee."

" Where I am, there ye shall be also."

" JESUS, the very thought of Thee,
     With sweetness fills my breast ;
But sweeter far Thy Face to see,
And in Thy presence rest."

" And they shall see His Face," " the
chief among ten thousand."

"I will come again, and receive you
unto Myself."

TO you is given to watch the coming
    of His Feet,
  Who is the glory of our Blessed
    Heaven !
The work and watching will be very
    sweet,
  Even in an earthly home,
And in such an hour as ye think not
  He will come."

"Even so ! come, Lord Jesus."

"Looking unto Jesus."

"O EYES that are weary,
    And hearts that are sore,
Look off unto Jesus,
    And sorrow no more!
The light of His countenance
    Shineth so bright,
That on Earth as in Heaven,
    There need be 'no night.'"

**"For He is our Peace." "And Christ
shall give thee Light."**

"I have loved thee with an Everlasting Love."

"THERE are who sigh that no fond
      heart is theirs:
   None loves them best! O vain and
      selfish sigh!
Out of the bosom of His Love He
      spares,   [to die!
   The Father spares the Son, for thee
For thee He died; for thee He lives
      again;
O'er thee He watches in His bound-
      less reign.
Thou art as much His care as if beside
   Nor man nor angel lived in heaven
      or earth.
Thus sunbeams pour alike their glori-
      ous tide
   To light up worlds, or wake an in-
      sect's mirth:
They shine and shine with unexhausted
      store,
Thou art *thy Saviour's darling*, — seek
      no more!"

I am my Beloved's, and my Beloved
      is mine."

"Fear none of those things which
thou shalt suffer."

"O COMFORTER of God's redeemed,
  Whom the world does not see,
What hand should pluck me from the
    flood
    That casts my soul on Thee?
Who would not suffer pain like mine,
  To be consoled like me?

"When I am feeble as a child,
  And flesh and heart give way,
Then on Thy everlasting strength
  With passive trust I stay;
And the rough wind becomes a song,
  The darkness shines like day."

"Strengthened with all might, accord
  ing to His glorious power, unto all
    patience and long suffering,
      with joyfulness." "Who
        teacheth like Him?"

"Bless the Lord, O my soul, and forget not all His benefits."

"TENDER mercies on my way,
    Falling softly like the dew,
Sent me freshly every day,
    Much I bless the Lord for you!

" Though I have not all I would,
    Though to greater bliss I go,
Every present gift of good
    To eternal love I owe!

" Source of all that comforts me,
    Well of joy for which I long,
Let the song I sing to Thee
    Be an everlasting song."

" Thanks be unto God for His un
speakable gift."

"Fear not, little flock;" "The very
hairs of your head are all numbered."

"LIVE for to-day; to-morrow's light
To-morrow's cares will bring to
sight !
Go, sleep like closing flowers at night,
And Heaven thy morn will bless."

"He that keepeth Israel shall neither
slumber nor sleep."

"Search me, O God, and know my heart." "The Lord knoweth them that are His."

"THOU knowest, Lord, the weariness
　　and sorrow
　　Of the sad heart that comes to Thee
　　for rest ;
Cares of to-day, and burdens for to-
　　morrow,
　　Blessings implored, and sins to be
　　confessed :
I come before Thee at Thy gracious
　　word,
And lay them at Thy feet ! Thou
　　knowest, Lord.

'Thou knowest not alone as God, all-
　　knowing ;
　　As man, our mortal weakness Thou
　　hast proved ;
On earth with purest sympathies o'er-
　　flowing,
　　O Saviour ! Thou hast wept, and
　　Thou hast loved.

And love and sorrow still to Thee may
 come,
And find a hiding-place, a rest, a
 home."

" For He was a Man of sorrows, and
acquainted with grief." " Come
unto Me, all ye that labour
and are heavy-laden, and
I will give you Rest."

" Peace I leave with you, My peace I
give unto you: not as the world
giveth, give I unto you "

" DOTH not Christ reach
His Hand of tenderness —
(Ah, precious, piercéd Hand which
once for sinners bled ;)
From Heaven down to earth, to lay it
on my head
In heavenly caress ? "

" The peace of God which passeth all
understanding, keep your heart
and mind."

"Thou shalt call His Name Jesus

" A LIVING, loving, lasting word,
     My listening ear believing, heard
While bending down in prayer:
Like a sweet breeze that none can stay
It passed my soul upon its way,
     And left a blessing there ;
And joyful thoughts that come and go
By paths the holy angels know,
     Encamped around my soul."

" For He shall save His people from
their sins."

"He that dwelleth in the secret place
of the Most High shall abide under
the shadow of the Almighty."

COME to me, Lord, to-night,
    And make Thy dwelling in my
    inmost heart,
That never more from Thee my soul
    may part,
    Its never-failing Light!

Under the shadow of Thy Wing
I'd make my Refuge, till the cares and
    fears
Of life are past; then through its tears,
    For joy, my soul shall sing!

"And sorrow and sighing shall flee
away!"

"I shall be satisfied when I awake
with Thy likeness."

"WHEN on the other side, thy feet
      Shall rest 'mid thousand wel-
   comes sweet,
One well-known Voice thy heart shall
      greet :
   '''Tis *I:* be not afraid.'

"From out the dazzling majesty,
   Gently He'll lay His Hand on thee,
Whispering, 'Beloved, lov'st thou Me?
'Twas not in vain I died for thee :
   'Tis *I:* be not afraid.'"

"Then were the disciples glad, when
   they saw the Lord."

"And God shall wipe away all tears
from their eyes."

WE have no tears Thou wilt not dry;
We have no wounds Thou wilt
not heal;
No sorrows pierce our human hearts
That Thou, dear Saviour, dost not
feel!

' Thy pity like the dew distils,
And Thy compassion like the light
Our every morning overfills,
And crowns with stars our every
night."

"Jesus wept!" "Behold how He
loved him."

"O! that I had wings like a dove
for then would I fly away and be
at rest."

'BEYOND the stars that shine in
   golden glory,
  Beyond the calm, sweet moon,
Up the bright ladder saints have trod
   before thee,
  Soul, thou shalt venture soon!
Secure with Him who sees thy heart-
   sick yearning,
  Safe in His arms of Love,
Thou shalt exchange the midnight for
   the morning,
  And thy fair home above!"

"Father, I will that they also whom
Thou hast given Me, be with Me
where I am."

"A little while and ye shall see me."

'SO I am watching quietly
    Every day;
Whenever the sun shines brightly,
    I rise and say,
'Surely it is the shining of His Face,'
And look to the gates of His high
    place
        Beyond the sea:
For I know He is coming shortly
    To summon me;
And when a shadow falls across the
    window of my room
Where I am working my appointed
    task,
I lift my head to watch the door, and
    ask
        If He is come?
And the Angel answers sweetly
    In my Home,
'Only a few more shadows,
    And He will come!'"

"And when she had thus said, she
turned herself back, and saw
Jesus."

" Having a desire to depart, and to be
with Christ."

" LIKE a bairn to its mither,
    A wee birdie to its nest,
I wad fain be ganging noo
    Unto my Saviour's breast.
For He gathers in His Arms,
Witless, worthless lambs like me,
And carries them Himsel' to His ain
    countree."

" Absent from the body, and to be
present with the Lord."

"When thou liest down, thou shalt
not be afraid: yea thou shalt lie
down, and thy sleep shall be
sweet."

SWEET is the solace of Thy Love,
   My heavenly Friend, to me,
While in the hidden way of faith
   I journey Home to Thee;
Learning in quiet thankfulness
   As Thy dear child to be."

" Who giveth songs in the night."

"And it came to pass, that as they
communed together, Jesus Himself
drew near and went with them."
" And they constrained Him saying,
'Abide with us, for it is toward
evening and the day is far spent.'"

"WE were talking about the King
    And our Elder Brother,
As we were used often to speak
    One to another.
The Lord standing quietly by
    In the shadows dim,
Smiling perhaps in the dark, to hear
    Our sweet, sweet talk of Him.

.   .   .   .

" 'I have come to call thee Home,'
    Said our veilèd Guest ;
'The terrible journey of Life is o'er,
    I will take thee into rest.'

.   .   .   .

And I knew by His loving voice,
    His kingly word,
The veilèd Guest in the starlight dim,
    Is Christ the Lord."

" This same Jesus "

"What time I am afraid I will trust in
Thee."

"THE way is dark, my child, but leads
to light;
I would not always have thee walk by
sight!
My dealings now thou canst not under-
stand;
I meant it so: but I will take thy hand,
And through the gloom
Lead safely home
My child!

'The path is rough, my child! but at
thy side
Thy Father walks: then be not terri-
fied,
For I am with thee; will thy foes com-
mand
To let thee freely pass: will take thy
hand,
And through the throng,
Lead safe along
My child!"

'Hold Thou me up, and I shall be
safe."

" The Lord preserveth all them that love Him."

' ANOTHER day is numbered with
the past,
Another night is given us for rest ;
Father, my spirit at Thy Feet I cast,
Oh, gather it unto Thy Loving Breast !

" Nightly Thou sendest rest to all the
earth,
Sendest a time for silence and returning ;
O Father ! teach me all the holy worth
Of the still hours when Thy clear
stars are burning."

**"I will meditate on Thee in the night-
watches."**

"Eye hath not seen, nor ear heard, neither have entered into the heart of man the things which God hath prepared for them that love Him."

"NO shadows yonder,
All light and song!
Each day I wonder,
And say how long
Shall time me sunder
From that dear throng?

"No partings yonder,
Time and space never
Again shall sunder;
Hearts cannot sever
Dearer and fonder
Hands clasp forever!"

"And they shall walk with Me in white, for they are worthy."
"And have washed their robes, and made them white in the blood of the Lamb."

582962

" Unto you which believe, He is precious."

" CLING to the Crucified!
　　His is a Heart of Love,
Full as the hearts above ;
Its depths of sympathy
Are all awake for thee !
His countenance is light
Even to the darkest night :
That Love shall never change,
　　That Light can ne'er grow dim :
Charge thou thy faithless heart
　　To find its all in Him !
　　　Cling to the Crucified ! "

" He is altogether lovely."

" To me, to live is Christ, and to die
is gain."

" DAWN is fair, because her mists
fade slowly
Into day, which floods the world
with light ;
Twilight's mystery is so deep and
holy,
Just because it ends in starry night.

" Life is only bright as it proceedeth
Toward a truer, deeper Life above ;
Human love is sweetest when it
leadeth
To a more divine and perfect love."

"For we shall see Him as He is."

"Though I walk through the valley
of the Shadow of Death I will fear
no evil: for Thou art with me: thy
rod and thy staff, they comfort me."

WHEN through the shadowed vale of
      death
I walk, why need I fear its gloom?
'T is only dark, because beyond
      So *brightly shines* my Heavenly Home.

     "And when on joyful wing
          Cleaving the sky,
      Sun, moon, and stars forgot,
          Upward I fly;
      Still all my song shall be, —
      Nearer my God to Thee,
          Nearer to Thee."

"Jesus said, I am the Resurrection
     and the Life."

"He will be very gracious unto thee
at the voice of thy cry: when
He shall hear it He will
answer thee."

" HERE is my heart! in Christ its
longings end,
Near to His Cross it draws :
It says, 'Thou art my portion, O my
Friend!
Thy blood my ransom was.'
And in the Saviour it has found
What blessedness and peace abound, —
My trusting heart.

" Here is my heart! ah, Holy Spirit
come,
Its nature to renew!
And consecrate it wholly as Thy Home,
A temple fair and true!
Teach it to love and serve Thee more,
To fear Thee, trust Thee, and adore,
My cleansed heart."

"As far as the east is from the west,
so far hath He removed our
transgressions from us."

" As thy days, so shall thy strength
be."

'TIS but a little while,
   Jesus hath said,
This shall my way beguile,
   And gladness shed ;
Then Thou Thyself wilt come,
Jesus, to take me home ;
   So let it be !

Home ! where my dear ones dwell,
   Gone on before !
Blest Home ! where all is well
   For evermore !
Home of the angels bright,
Home of the saints of light,
   Home of my God !

" And everlasting joy shall be upon
their head : they shall obtain glad-
ness and joy : and sorrow and
mourning shall flee away."

"He giveth His Beloved sleep."

'SLEEP, soft beloved," we sometimes
say,
But have no tune to charm away
   Sad dreams that through the eyelids
   creep;
But never doleful dream again
Shall break the happy slumber, when
  "*He giveth His Beloved* sleep."

"Sleep in Jesus."

"Thy sun shall no more go down,
neither shall thy moon withdraw
itself; the Lord shall be thine everlasting Light, and the days of thy
mourning shall be ended."

"GOOD-NIGHT;" now cometh gen-
tle sleep,
And dreams that fall like gentle rain;
Good-night! oh, holy, blessed, and deep
The rest that follows pain :
How should we reach God's upper
Light
If life's long day had no "Good-night."

"And they that be wise shall be as
the firmament," "as the stars
forever and ever."
"And the Lamb is the Light thereof."

www.ingramcontent.com/pod-product-compliance
Lightning Source LLC
Chambersburg PA
CBHW020034030726
47499CB00007B/2415